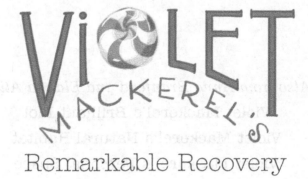

Remarkable Recovery

VIOLET MACKEREL'S

Remarkable Recovery

Anna Branford

illustrated by

Elanna Allen

A
atheneum

Atheneum Books for Young Readers
New York   London   Toronto   Sydney   New Delhi

𝒜
atheneum

Atheneum Books for Young Readers
An imprint of Simon & Schuster Children's Publishing Division
1230 Avenue of the Americas, New York, New York 10020
Text was originally published in 2011 by Walker Books Australia Pty Ltd.
For information about special discounts for bulk purchases, please contact Simon & Schuster Special Sales at 1-866-506-1949 or business@simonandschuster.com.
The Simon & Schuster Speakers Bureau can bring authors to your live event. For more information or to book an event, contact the Simon & Schuster Speakers Bureau at 1-866-248-3049 or visit our website at www.simonspeakers.com.
Also available in an Atheneum Books for Young Readers hardcover edition
Book design by Lauren Rille
The text for this book is set in Excelsior.
The illustrations for this book are rendered in pencil with digital ink.
Manufactured in the United States of America
0219 MTN

10 9 8 7
Library of Congress Cataloging-in-Publication Data
Branford, Anna.
Violet Mackerel's remarkable recovery / Anna Branford ; illustrated by Elanna Allen.
p. cm.
Summary: With her knack for seeing the positive, six-year-old Violet anticipates extraordinary results after getting her tonsils removed, such as making a special new friend and turning her everyday voice into an opera voice.
ISBN 978-1-4424-3588-9 (hc)— ISBN 978-1-4424-3589-6 (pbk.)
ISBN 978-1-4424-3590-2 (eBook)
[1. Friendship—Fiction. 2. Sick—Fiction. 3. Tonsillectomy—Fiction.]
I. Allen, Elanna, ill. II. Title.
PZ7.B737384Vi 2012
[Fic]—dc23 2011023703

For Rusty
(my dad)
— A. B.

For Mumzi
— E. A.

Remarkable Recovery

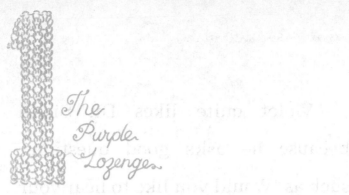

1
The Purple Lozenges

Violet Mackerel has an extremely sore throat.

It feels awful to talk, terrible to swallow, and horrible to eat.

Her older sister, Nicola, and her brother, Dylan, have just left for school. Violet has been home from school all week, and today Mama is taking her to see Dr. Singh.

Violet quite likes Dr. Singh because he asks good questions, such as "Would you like to hear your heartbeat through my stethoscope?" and "Do you want to see how my examination table goes up and down?"

Also, if you meet him for the first time when you are only five years old, and you wonder, since his name sounds like "sing," if he might be a singing sort of doctor, he doesn't mind making up a little tune such as:

GOOD MORNING, VIOLET MACKEREL! AND HOW ARE YOU TODAY? THAT'S QUITE A NASTY BRUISE YOU HAVE, BUT IT SHOULD FADE AWAY!

When Violet and Mama get to the doctor's office, they sit in the waiting room. Mama knits a few rows of a soft, rosy cardigan. She is a very good knitter.

Soon the lady at the desk says, "Violet Mackerel," which means it is time for Violet and Mama to go and see Dr. Singh.

"How are you this morning?" he asks, feeling her forehead.

"My throat hurts," croaks Violet, "and it feels as if there is a cactus in it."

Dr. Singh presses a big, flat Popsicle stick on her tongue.

"Say ahhhh," he says.

"Ahhhh," says Violet.

4

"And again," says Dr. Singh.

"Ahhhh," says Violet.

"Hmm," says Dr. Singh, who has been looking down Violet's throat. "I'm afraid that's a bad case of tonsillitis."

Violet has had tonsillitis before. It is when two bits at the back of your throat, which are called tonsils, swell up and feel as though you have swallowed a cactus.

"I'll give you some lozenges for now, to help with the prickles," says

Dr. Singh, "but I think it would be a good idea to have your tonsils taken out."

Violet, however, does *not* think this is a good idea. She generally prefers *not* to have things taken out.

"It's a very simple operation," explains Dr. Singh, "and you'll be asleep all the way through it. And then you'll need a while at home afterward, resting and eating ice cream."

Violet has never been in the hospital before and she quite likes ice cream.

"Anything else?" she asks.

Dr. Singh thinks.

"Well," he says, "some people find that their voices change a little bit after they have their tonsils out."

This is very interesting to Violet, who always thinks about singing when she sees Dr. Singh, even though she knows now that he is not really a singing sort of doctor.

Violet thinks how exciting it would be if, when she was singing in the bath, her voice carried down

into the garden and all the way along
the street. The neighbors would say,
"Who is doing that lovely opera
singing?" and Mama would say, "Oh,
that is Violet. She always sings like
that since she had her tonsils out

and soon she is going to be a real opera singer on the radio."

"How soon could I be an opera singer on the radio?" croaks Violet.

"Well, most people feel completely better in a couple of weeks," says Dr. Singh. "I'm not sure about opera singing, but I have certainly seen some remarkable recoveries in my time."

Violet decides that hers will be the most remarkable recovery Dr. Singh has *ever* seen in his time.

"Until then," he says, "would you like pink throat lozenges that taste like strawberries, or purple throat lozenges that taste like grapes?"

Violet thinks it is an excellent question.

"Purple, please," she says.

Dr. Singh pops open a packet of lozenges and gives one to Violet so it can start soothing her throat prickles

right away. The purple lozenge looks

like a precious crystal in her palm.

And it gives Violet an idea.

2 The Perfect Violet

On the drive home Violet's idea is slowly growing into a theory. It is called The Theory of Giving Small Things, and it works like this: If someone has a problem and you give them something small, like a feather, or a pebble, or a purple lozenge, that small thing might have a strange and special way of helping them.

Of course, it might help in an ordinary way. For example, handkerchiefs are helpful for runny noses, Band-Aids are good for grazed knees, and purple lozenges are excellent when you have tonsillitis.

But the small thing might also help in an *extraordinary* way, and that is the interesting part.

Violet suspects, for example, that when Dr. Singh

gave her that purple lozenge, there
was, tucked inside it, a little bit of
the singing part of his name, which
will be very helpful for turning her
everyday voice into an opera voice.
She also suspects that when Vincent

picks a flower for Mama, it is not just the flower but a sort of special wish tucked somewhere inside it that makes Mama have such a nice smile. (Vincent is Mama's boyfriend. He comes to their house a lot and he quite often picks Mama a flower on the way.)

"You're very quiet," says Mama to Violet. "Are you a bit worried about going to the hospital?"

"Maybe a bit," says Violet. "Have you ever been to the hospital?"

"Well," says Mama, "the last time I went to the hospital was when you were being born."

"Were you nervous?"

"Maybe, but I think I was too excited to notice," says Mama.

That is a bit how Violet feels too.

In a photo album at Violet's

house there is a picture from just after Violet was born. In it, she looks a bit like a tiny, pink, hairy monkey wrapped in one of Mama's knitted blankets. Mama looks very tired and there are teardrops on her cheeks, but she has the look on her face of birthdays and Christmases all at once. It is Violet's favorite photo.

"Did you know I was going to be a girl called Violet?" asks Violet.

"We knew you were going to be a girl," says Mama, "but at first, no one could think of a name for you."

"Why did you decide to call me Violet?" asks Violet.

"Well, after you were born, the midwife gave me a perfect violet for

the little vase by my bed. That's what
gave me the idea."

Violet smiles.

"Would you have called me Rose
if the midwife had picked you a perfect rose?"

"Maybe," says Mama.

"Would you have called me Daffodil if she had picked you a perfect daffodil?"

"Probably not," says Mama.

Violet is quite glad that the midwife gave Mama a perfect violet. A violet is a very small flower. It must have been just the right sort of small thing to help Mama when she was tired after having a baby and needed to think of a good name.

"I'm not nervous about having

my tonsils out," says Violet. "Not really."

Then her throat is too prickly for any more talking.

3 The New Verses

Over the next few days, Violet finds out another interesting thing about having your tonsils out, which is that the proper name for it is "tonsillectomy."

The day before her trip to the hospital, the postman comes to Violet's house to deliver a box of wool to Mama.

"I'm having a tonsillectomy

tomorrow," Violet tells him. She wonders if he will be a little bit jealous about the ice cream and the change of voice.

"A tonsillectomy? You brave little thing!" he says.

Then, later on, a lady comes to the door asking Mama to sign a petition.

"I'm having a tonsillectomy tomorrow," Violet tells her.

"A tonsillectomy? Goodness me!" says the lady, clucking and tutting.

No one seems to be at all jealous. But it is quite interesting to have so much clucking and tutting and people saying "goodness me."

In the evening, Vincent cooks dinner for everyone. Violet looks down at the kitchen floor and sighs very deeply. She hopes Vincent will ask her what is wrong, but he is a bit deaf, and anyway, there is a very loud noise of French fries sizzling in the pan.

She sighs much more loudly.

Still nothing.

"I am having a tonsillectomy tomorrow," says Violet. She tries to sniffle a little bit.

"I know," says Vincent. "You get to stay in bed and eat ice cream for a week. I'm jealous."

Violet smiles.

"I am going to have a remarkable recovery," she tells Vincent. "When you hear me singing in the bath, you won't even know it's me. You will have to ask Mama who is doing that lovely opera singing, and Mama will say, 'It is Violet, and soon she will be on the radio.'"

Violet has been making up a

verse for a song she likes called "My Favorite Things." It is from a movie about children with a nice nanny, and Violet likes making up new verses for it. Her newest verse goes like this:

Big chunky markers and

aprons with pockets

Movies with planets and

spacemen and rockets

Small purple lozenges

from Dr. Singh's

These are a few of my

favorite things

Violet wishes she could sing it for Vincent and Mama, but her throat is too sore.

Before she goes to sleep, Violet says good night to her tonsils.

4
The Waiting Room

The next morning Violet wakes up with a strange feeling inside her. It is called butterflies, which is odd, Violets thinks, since it feels so much more like rhinoceroses.

Violet can't have any breakfast because you're not supposed to eat before you have an operation. There is a nice smell of toast coming from the kitchen. The smell makes the rhinoceroses stamp around crossly inside Violet.

Mama is in her bedroom getting dressed, and Violet goes in for a chat.

"I've changed my mind," says Violet. "I'm going to keep my tonsils and have some toast."

"That's a shame," says Mama. "Vincent brought so much ice cream over that I can hardly close the door of the freezer."

"All the same flavor?" asks Violet.

"All different flavors," says Mama.

Violet thinks.

"Also," says Mama, "I was looking forward to hearing the next verse of 'My Favorite Things' being sung in your new voice."

Violet had been looking forward
to that too.

So Violet takes a very deep breath and thinks that maybe she will still have the tonsillectomy after all.

She packs a small bag to take to the hospital. First she packs some ordinary things, like a book and a teddy. Then she packs some other things. One is a Blue China Bird that Vincent gave her, because she feels it may have some of Vincent's braveness tucked inside it. Vincent has been backpacking all over the world and that is the sort of braveness that is very useful when you are having a tonsillectomy.

Next she packs a woolly scarf that Mama made for her, because she feels it might have a sort of hug tucked in it, which might be helpful if you need to make a remarkable recovery.

And finally she packs a "get well soon" card that her big brother,

Dylan, made for her, which has a picture of her singing in the opera with lots of musical notes coming out of her mouth. Dylan is a very good violin player, and Violet feels he may have tucked some musical genius into the card, which is just the sort of thing that helps when you want to sing opera on the radio.

After Nicola and Dylan have gone to school, Mama puts a

big basket of wool and needles in the trunk of the car so she can do some knitting while Violet is having her operation. Violet puts her bag beside it and then they are ready to go.

On the way, Violet tries to think of some new words for "My Favorite Things," but the rhinoceroses keep distracting her.

The waiting room at the hospital is bigger than at Dr. Singh's. One of the people waiting there is an old lady sitting by herself. She looks as though she has been waiting for a very long time. Mama notices her too.

"I feel as though I've seen her somewhere before," whispers Mama to Violet.

The old lady has a green cardigan and a necklace of bright red beads and she is doing a funny thing with her hands. Her fingers, which have lots of rings on them, are all laced together and she is making her thumbs go round and round.

Violet tries it, but it is trickier than it looks.

"Are you having a tonsillectomy?" Violet asks the old lady.

The old lady smiles. "No, I'm having an operation on my arm," she says.

"Do you have butterflies?" asks Violet.

"Well, *I* think they feel more like rhinoceroses," says the old lady.

Violet smiles.

5 *The Old Lady*

While they wait, the old lady in the waiting room shows Violet how to do the trick with her thumbs and Violet shows the old lady the things in her bag. The old lady especially likes the Blue China Bird.

"It reminds me of my garden when I was a little girl in England," she says. "There were robins in the winter and their eggs were just that color."

"Do you have a garden now?" asks Violet.

"Yes," says the old lady, "though lately my arm has been too sore to do much gardening. But when I can garden, I grow beautiful flowers."

"After your arm operation, will you be able to grow them again?"

"I hope so," says the old lady.

"Dr. Singh says that

after my tonsillectomy my voice will change a bit," Violet tells the lady. "Right now I have an ordinary voice, but afterward I think it will change into an opera voice."

"Really?" asks the old lady.

"Yes," says Violet. "You'll probably hear me on the radio sometime. My name is Violet Mackerel, just so you can be sure it is me. And maybe after *your* operation, your ordinary arm will turn into a superarm.

Then you will be able to do lots of gardening and lots of other things, too. When the other old ladies can't get the lids off their jars, they will bring them to your house and you'll be able to do it on the first try."

The old lady laughs a little bit. "It *would* be handy to have a super-arm," she says.

Violet wishes she had a small thing to give her, to help. She asks Mama if there are any more purple lozenges.

"I don't think you should have one right before your operation," says Mama.

"It's not for me," says Violet. Mama gives her a purple lozenge.

Violet wraps up the purple lozenge in a tissue like a present and gives it to the old lady. She explains the Theory of Giving Small Things and tells her about how, tucked inside the purple lozenge, there could be a little bit of Violet's own superness.

"Thank you," says the old lady.

Then a man comes out and says in a loud voice, "IRIS MACDONALD."

"That's me," says the old lady.

"How are your rhinoceroses?" asks Violet.

"They're not too bad now, actually," says the old lady, putting the purple lozenge in her cardigan pocket. "It was lovely to meet you," she says to Violet.

"It was lovely to meet you, too," says Violet, "and when we have both had remarkable recoveries, I think we should have tea together so you can hear my opera voice and I can see your superarm."

"Let's do that," says the old lady.

"Promise?" asks Violet.

"I promise," says the old lady Iris MacDonald.

They wave good-bye.

Violet's rhinoceroses aren't too bad now either.

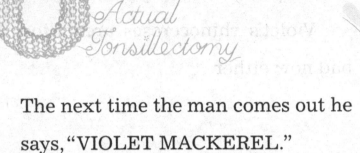

6 The Actual Tonsillectomy

The next time the man comes out he says, "VIOLET MACKEREL."

Violet and Mama pack up their things and follow him down a little corridor. They meet another doctor and a nurse and the nurse shows Violet the bed that will be hers while she is in the hospital. The mattress is a bit thin-
ner than her

bed at home, but it is as white as a cloud and Violet quite likes it.

She does not at all like the part where they give her a needle and it feels like a sharp little pinch on her arm, but it is over very, very quickly and then she drifts off to sleep.

Violet sleeps right through the tonsillectomy and when she wakes up, still on her cloud bed, Mama is there and the tonsillectomy is finished.

"Hello," says Mama, smiling. "How are you feeling?"

"A bit groggy," croaks Violet.

She sleeps a bit more with Mama next to her and then she wakes up again and watches Mama knitting for a while. It is a nice thing to see while you are drowsing after a tonsillectomy.

Soon she feels well enough to sit up, and Mama has a cup of tea and Violet has some ice to suck. And then it is only a bit more time until the nurse says Violet is well enough to go home.

When she gets home, Violet is still feeling groggy, so she goes back to bed with a hot water bottle, even though it is still daytime. Her big sister, Nicola, who is a very good jewelry maker, has made her a beautiful necklace. The beads have little letters of the alphabet on them and they spell out "g-e-t-w-e-l-l-s-o-o-n-v-i-o-l-e-t." It is in a little box by Violet's bed.

Violet drifts in and out
of sleep and has strange
dreams of butterflies
with rhinoceros horns and
rhinoceroses with butterfly
wings, and rhinocerflies
and butternocer-
oses with necklaces
that say "g-e-t-w-
e-l-l-s-o-o-n." Mama
and Nicola and Dylan
and Vincent come in
and say "hello"

and "how are you feeling?," but Violet is too sleepy and groggy to say too much back.

The next morning, though, she feels a bit better. Mama has to go out to a special knitting workshop, so Vincent comes round to look after Violet and they eat minty ice cream with pink bits and watch the movie about the children and the nanny with the song "My Favorite Things."

Then Violet feels floppy again, so Vincent refills her hot water bottle and they listen to some opera music on the radio.

"My throat feels funny and I still feel

a bit groggy," says Violet. "Do you think that means my recovery isn't going to be very remarkable?"

"No," says Vincent. "I think even very remarkable recoveries probably take a few days."

"I think so too," says Violet, who is drifting off again.

When she wakes up, Vincent has gone home and Mama is back from the knitting workshop. She tries to refill Violet's water bottle, but Vincent has twisted the top on so tightly that she can't get it off. After a little while her face is all red from trying.

"It's no good," she says. "My arm isn't strong enough."

And then, suddenly, Violet remembers the old lady Iris MacDonald.

7 The Totbafin Plot

"How are we going to find Iris MacDonald?" asks Violet.

"Who?" says Mama.

"The old lady Iris MacDonald *promised* we would have tea when we were better, so she could hear my opera voice and I could see her superarm. But she doesn't have our phone number and we don't have hers, so how will we be able to have tea with her?"

Mama thinks.

"She knows my name is Violet Mackerel," says Violet, "and there aren't many other Mackerels in the phone book, so maybe she will look us up."

"She might," says Mama.

"But what if she doesn't quite remember my name?" asks Violet. "What if she remembers Violet, but not quite Mackerel?"

"Well . . . ," begins Mama.

"Let's phone the hospital and ask them and tell them it is an emergency," says Violet.

"I don't think this is really the sort of emergency that hospitals help with," says Mama.

Mama thinks a bit more.

"Violet, it *might* be that Iris MacDonald was just a friend for the time you were in the hospital waiting room and not really the sort of friend for having tea with afterward."

This suggestion of Mama's makes Violet feel quite cross. Her throat is too sore from her tonsillectomy to have a cross voice, so instead she frowns until her eyebrows almost get in her eyes.

"Iris MacDonald is *not* that kind of friend," she says to Mama.

Violet frowns more. Frowning is not as good as a cross voice, which people have to hear whether they want to or not. People have to be

looking right at you to see how hard you are frowning, and Mama is not looking.

"Please can I have a notebook?" Violet asks Mama when her eyebrows are too tired to frown anymore.

Mama brings a bowl of frosty forest-berry ice cream, a notebook, and a pencil on a tray to Violet's bed, and Violet starts a new page that is called Thinking Outside the Box About Finding Iris MacDonald.

"Thinking outside the box" is when you find extraordinary solutions to problems and puzzles, because extraordinary solutions are often better than the ordinary sort. It is one of Violet's favorite problem-solving strategies.

In parentheses, after "Thinking Outside the Box About Finding Iris MacDonald," Violet writes "The Totbafim Plot." The word "Totbafim" is made from the first letters of all the words in her plot.

Thinking Outside the Box About
Finding Iris MacDonald (The TOTBAFIM Plot)

Next on the page she draws a big
box, and inside the box she writes
her ordinary ideas, such as:

Ask everyone we know if
they know a nice old lady
called Iris MacDonald.

and

Ask everyone we know to
ask everyone they know

If they know a nice old lady called Iris MacDonald.

Then outside the box she writes her extraordinary ideas, such as:

Hire one of those little airplanes that can write things in clouds in the sky and write, "If your name is Iris MacDonald, please could you ring up Violet Mackerel?"

and

Put an advertisement in
the Lost and Found section
of the newspaper that says,
"Lost: one old lady called
Iris MacDonald with a
superarm."

They are all good ideas, Violet
thinks, especially the ones outside
the box.

But it is very difficult to make
any of them happen from your bed,

where you are still recovering from a
tonsillectomy.

That is the problem.

8

The Star Message

That night before bed, while she is eating ginger and passion fruit ice cream, Violet feels a bit sad.

She asks Dylan if he will help her to find the old lady Iris MacDonald, and he says he will put a little notice about her in his violin case. Dylan plays his violin at the market on Saturday mornings, and people throw coins in his case. He thinks they might read a little notice if there was one there.

Violet is not sure.

Violet also asks Nicola if she will help her to find the old lady Iris MacDonald, and Nicola says she will put up a sign on the notice board at school.

"I don't think Iris MacDonald will see it there," says Violet.

Violet says thank you to her brother and sister for trying, but before she goes to sleep she decides that she will ring up Vincent and see if he has any ideas. Violet knows Vincent's phone number and she can dial it by herself.

"The Totbafim Plot didn't work," Violet tells him.

"The Totbafim Plot," says Vincent thoughtfully. "What's that?"

"It was the plan to help me find the old lady Iris MacDonald who I met in the hospital waiting room."

"If it *had* worked and you *had* found her, what would you have said?" asks Vincent.

Violet thinks.

"'I hope your arm is feeling better and I am glad we got to be friends in the waiting room,'" she says.

Violet is surprised that it isn't a

message about the opera voice and the superarm, or even the afternoon tea. Sometimes you don't even know what you think until someone asks you a question like that.

"When you are a backpacker like me," says Vincent, "you meet lots and lots of special people just once, and never get to see them again. So what I do, sometimes, is send messages to the stars for them."

"Do they get your messages?" asks Violet.

"I don't know," says Vincent. "But maybe they feel something special when they look at the stars that night."

It is a good idea, Violet thinks.

She says good night to Vincent and she looks out at the stars through her bedroom window. She rests her hands on the windowsill and circles her thumbs in the way of the old lady Iris MacDonald.

"This is a message for Iris MacDonald," says Violet to the stars as her thumbs go round and round.

Thank you for being my friend in the waiting room and I hope your arm is getting better. Even very remarkable recoveries can take a few days, so don't worry if your arm is not super yet. Lots of love from Violet Mackerel. (There are not many Mackerels in the phone book, so if you want to look me up, you still can.)

That night in bed, before she goes to sleep, Violet composes a verse

of "My Favorite Things" especially in honor of the old lady Iris MacDonald. After that, she feels a bit better.

9 The Gardening Channel

In the morning, while she has her purple, yogurt, grape-and-blueberry breakfast ice cream, Violet listens to the radio. Most of all she would like to hear some opera music. She likes thinking of the radio host saying, "And that was Violet Mackerel, who never sang like that before her tonsillectomy." But this morning there is no opera music on any of the radio stations.

So Violet decides that she will listen to the Gardening Channel, since somebody has rung in to ask a question about violets.

"The leaves on my violets have dead spots. I've tried everything, but it just keeps on happening," says the caller.

"Hmm," says the host of the Gardening Channel. "I'm afraid I don't know much about growing violets, but if any of our listeners have any ideas, we'd love to hear from you."

Violet wishes she knew the answer to the problem. She would quite like to ring up and talk on the radio. She listens to a few more questions, but they're not about violets so they're not so interesting.

Then a lady rings up who says she has an answer to the violet question, so Violet listens carefully again.

"It sounds like a problem with watering," says the lady. "The trick with watering violets is to do it from underneath, not from above. They much prefer to sit in water for a little while than be sprinkled and get water on their leaves."

There is something very familiar about her voice.

"Thank you for calling. You've been very helpful," says the radio host. "What was your name?"

"Iris MacDonald," says the lady.

"MAMA!" yells Violet, too excited to notice that she is yelling and her throat is feeling better,

THE OLD LADY Iris MacDonald is on the radio!

Mama is not as excited as Violet, which is partly because she sloshed tea down her dressing gown when she heard Violet yelling and rushed up the stairs to see if she was being eaten by an escaped zoo animal.

The next time the radio host gives the telephone number for the Gardening Channel, Violet writes it down in her notebook. Then she picks up the phone and dials.

"Hello," says the radio host. "Can you answer any of our gardening questions this morning?"

Violet thinks.

"I agree about watering the violets," she says. "I am a Violet and I much prefer sitting in the bath to being sprinkled in the shower."

"I see," says the radio host.

"But that is not why I called," says Violet. "I called because I met Iris MacDonald in the hospital waiting room when I was having my tonsillectomy."

It is funny for Violet to hear her own voice talking on the radio as well as through the phone.

"I see," says the radio host again, but he sounds as though he doesn't *quite* see.

"We were supposed to have tea

together, so I could see her superarm and she could hear my opera singing voice," says Violet. "I am going to be an opera singer on the radio," she explains.

"Well," says the radio host, "you're on the radio now. Would you like to sing a song for Iris?"

"Yes please," says Violet.

She pauses for a moment just to make sure Iris MacDonald will have time to get nice and close to her radio.

red beads and cardigans
made of green knitting
round-and-round thumbs
while you're quietly sitting

robins' eggs, flowers,
and fingers with rings

these are a few of Iris
MacDonald's favorite
thiiiiings

When she sings "thiiiiiings," Violet jiggles a little bit, and her voice *does* sound a lot like an opera singer's.

"That was lovely," says the host. "Thank you very much for calling, Violet."

"You're welcome," says Violet.

A little while later the phone rings and it is someone from the Gardening Channel with a message for Violet and Mama from Iris MacDonald. The message is

Violet Mackerel's Remarkable Recovery

an invitation for tea tomorrow at eleven o'clock.

This time Violet carefully writes down all the details.

10 The Super Arm

Just when Violet is thinking that eleven o'clock tomorrow will never, ever come, it finally does.

To get to the front door of Iris MacDonald's house you have to walk through some of her garden, and it is very beautiful. There is even a violet patch, with no spots on the leaves. They ring the doorbell and Iris MacDonald answers it. Her arm is in a plaster cast in a sling, which makes hugs tricky, but she and Violet manage anyway.

"Thank you very much for inviting us," says Mama.

"Thank you for coming," says Iris MacDonald. "I was so disappointed when I realized we'd parted without exchanging phone numbers. I couldn't think how I was going to keep my promise!"

Violet does not say, "I told you so," but she does raise her eyebrows just a little bit at Mama.

Iris MacDonald has a cake with lemon icing and a pot of tea, and there are rosy teacups on saucers. Violet and Mama help her to carry it

all out from the kitchen, as it is difficult to carry lots of things at once if
you are only using one arm. They sit
down in the living room and Violet
looks at all the little ornaments on
the shelves and wonders if they are
all small gifts with hidden helpful-
ness tucked inside them.

"Now," says Iris MacDonald when she has had some cake. "Even though I am older than seventy, I have never had a song written for me before. Do you think I could hear that lovely verse again?"

"Yes," says Violet, and she sings "Iris MacDonald's Favorite Things," jiggling on the final "thiiiiiiings" like a real opera singer.

"I love it," says Iris MacDonald. "And I can't believe how many of my favorite things you managed to squeeze in."

Violet smiles. "What about your arm?" she asks. "Is it starting to feel super yet?"

"Not really," says Iris MacDonald. "I still keep your purple lozenge in my pocket, just in case. But if you like, I will tell you and your mama a secret about my arm."

Violet and Mama listen very carefully, because they both quite like secrets.

"The real truth," whispers Iris MacDonald, "is that both of

my arms are pretty special. For all of
my working life I have been a midwife, so I have helped hundreds and
hundreds and *hundreds* of
mothers to give birth.
That means my arms

have been the first arms to hold hundreds and hundreds and *hundreds* of new babies. In fact, some of the babies I've helped to deliver have grown up and come back so I can help them deliver *their* babies."

Violet is just thinking what a good secret it is when Mama does a cough like a small explosion into her cup of tea.

"I knew I'd seen you somewhere before," squeaks Mama. "You were my midwife when I gave birth to Violet! We chose her name because of the perfect violet you gave me afterward."

The old lady Iris MacDonald's face has the smile of someone who is not very old at all.

"I often took flowers from my garden to give to the new mothers," she says.

Violet can hardly believe it.

"I have *never* met anyone with

arms like yours before," she says.

"And I have never met a real opera singer who sings on the radio before," says Iris MacDonald.

Before Violet goes home, Iris MacDonald gives her a little envelope and in it is a card that says:

Dear Violet,
Congratulations on your
remarkable recovery.
With love from
Iris MacDonald
x x x

And tucked inside it is another perfect violet.